"May the guns fall silent
at least upon the night the angels sang."

Pope Benedict XV's
plea for an official ceasefire
Christmas 1914.

Stille
heilige
Alles
einsam

Nacht, Nacht, schläft, wacht.

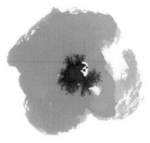

This book is dedicated to Two Brave Lions who survived
The Great War.

Charles Norman James
"Jimmy"
Bomber Pilot RFC
Jimmy was the Great Grandfather of
Patrick Watson
aged 11

"He was as brave as a lion!"
PW

Thomas Higgs
Royal Army Medical Corp
Thomas was the Great Great Grandfather of
Lewie Higgs
aged 5

"I am very proud."
LH

Patrick and Lewie were winners of a competition
to dedicate this book to a hero of the First World War.
The competition, to mark the Centenary of the Christmas Truce 1914,
was coordinated and judged by Seven Stories, National Centre for Children's Books, Newcastle, UK.

first edition

STRAUSS HOUSE PRODUCTIONS
www.strausshouseproductions.com

First published in Great Britain 2014
Text copyright © Hilary Robinson 2014
Illustrations copyright © Martin Impey 2014
Hilary Robinson and Martin Impey have asserted their rights
to be identified as the author and illustrator of this work under
The Copyright, Designs and Patents Act, 1988
British Library Cataloguing in Publication Data
A catalogue record for this book is available from the British Library
All rights reserved. ISBN - 978-0-9571245-7-8
Printed in the UK

The Christmas Truce

The Place Where Peace Was Found

by

Hilary Robinson and Martin Impey

STRAUSS HOUSE
PRODUCTIONS

This is the place where peace was found.

This is the moon, shining bright,
That lit up the place where peace was found.

These are the soldiers, watching by night,
Under the moon, shining bright,
That lit up the place where peace was found.

This is Karl and his best friend Lars
Who sang *Silent Night* under the stars
To enemy soldiers, watching by night,
Under the moon, shining bright,
That lit up the place where peace was found.

This is Ray and his best friend Ben,
Two of the soldiers who listened when
Karl stood up with his friend Lars
And sang *Silent Night* under the stars
To enemy soldiers, watching by night,
Under the moon, shining bright,
That lit up the place where peace was found.

These are the men who held out a hand,
A sign of peace in No Man's Land,
To men like Ray and his friend Ben,
Two of the soldiers who listened when
Karl stood up with his friend Lars
And sang *Silent Night* under the stars
To enemy soldiers, watching by night,
Under the moon, shining bright,
That lit up the place where peace was found.

These are the bells that started to chime
When friends were made at Christmas time,
When enemy soldiers held out a hand,
A sign of peace in No Man's Land,
Peace for men like Ray and Ben,
Two of the soldiers who listened when
Karl stood up with his friend Lars
And sang *Silent Night* under the stars
To enemy soldiers, watching by night,
Under the moon, shining bright,
That lit up the place where peace was found.

This is the football match that was played
As over the hills evergreens swayed
To echoes of bells that started to chime
When friends were made at Christmas time,
When enemy soldiers held out a hand,
A sign of peace in No Man's Land,
Peace for men like Ray and Ben,
Two of the soldiers who listened when
Karl stood up with his friend Lars
And sang *Silent Night* under the stars
To enemy soldiers, watching by night,
Under the moon, shining bright,
That lit up the place where peace was found.

This is the dove that flew above,
A symbol of enduring love,
Who honoured the place the match was played
As over the hills evergreens swayed
To echoes of bells that started to chime
When friends were made at Christmas time,
When enemy soldiers held out a hand,
A sign of peace in No Man's Land,
Peace for men like Ray and Ben,
Two of the soldiers who listened when
Karl stood up with his friend Lars
And sang *Silent Night* under the stars
To enemy soldiers, watching by night,
Under the moon, shining bright,
That lit up the place where peace was found.

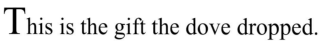

This is the gift the dove dropped.

This is the olive branch that was dropped
On Christmas Day when fighting stopped,
Dropped by a dove flying above,
A symbol of enduring love,
Who honoured the place the match was played
As over the hills evergreens swayed
To echoes of bells that started to chime
When friends were made at Christmas time,
When enemy soldiers held out a hand,
A sign of peace in No Man's Land,
Peace for men like Ray and Ben,
Two of the soldiers who listened when
Karl stood up with his friend Lars
And sang *Silent Night* under the stars
To enemy soldiers, watching by night,
Under the moon, shining bright,
That lit up the place
that Christmas day...

...where peace was found.

PEACE

PLUGSTREET 1914
THE PLACE WHERE PEACE WAS FOUND

WHERE THE POPPIES NOW GROW

Stille Nacht, heilige Nacht,

Thank you
Jackie Hamley, Jim Millea, Megan Brownrigg, Gary Brandham,
Justin Leeming, The Castleford Male Voice Choir,
Hannah Lambert, Seven Stories, National Centre for Children's Books,
Robin Schäfer (gottmituns-consult.com), Paul Reed (ww1revisited.com),
Sir John & Lady Frances Sorrell, Joke de Winter,
Nerys Spofforth, Cathi Poole, Nicky Stonehill, Jessica Ward,
Charles Timberlake, John Daniels, Anthony Richards, Alan Wakefield
and a very special *'Thank you'* to Andrew Robinson and Emilie James.

The Place Where Peace Was Found

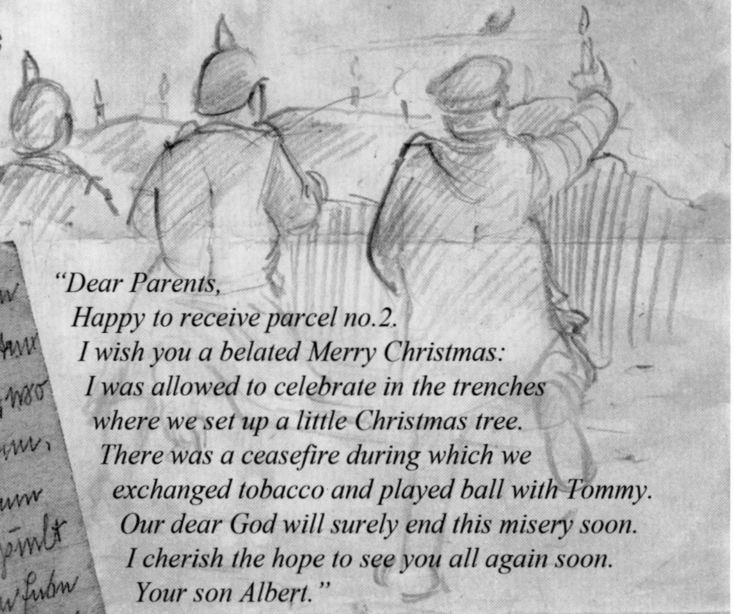

Letter from a German Soldier
15th Jan 1915 *

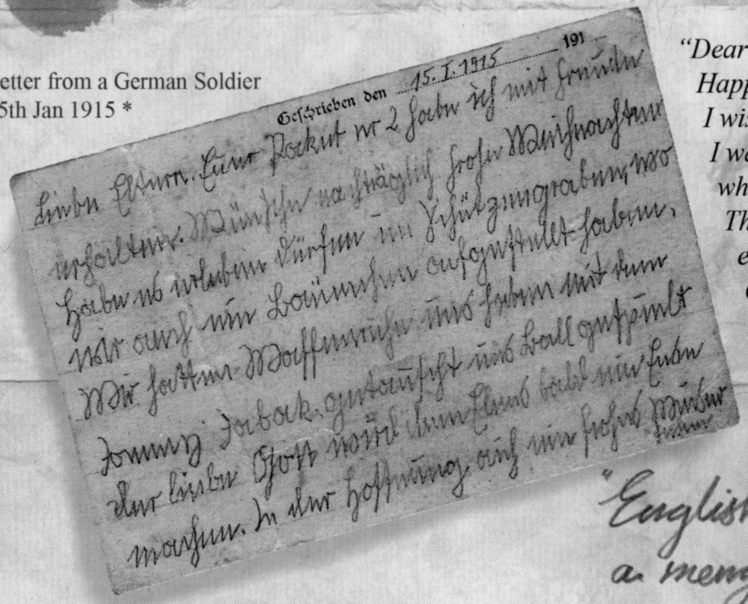

Geschrieben den 15.1.1915 191

[German handwritten letter]

"Dear Parents,
Happy to receive parcel no.2.
I wish you a belated Merry Christmas:
I was allowed to celebrate in the trenches
where we set up a little Christmas tree.
There was a ceasefire during which we
exchanged tobacco and played ball with Tommy.
Our dear God will surely end this misery soon.
I cherish the hope to see you all again soon.
Your son Albert."

* Horst and Robin Schäfer, private collection, Germany.

"English soldiers, English soldiers,
a merry Christmas,
a merry Christmas."

2 GERMANS ADVANCED UNARMED TOWARDS
OUR TRENCHES AND OUR MEN DID THE
SAME. THEY MET HALF WAY AND SHOOK HANDS...

Rifleman Jack Chappell - 1/5th Londons ***

A light in the enemy's trenches
was so rare at that hour...
light after light sprang up along
the German front...
... a few of us advanced to meet
the on-coming Germans...
Out went the hands and tightened
in the grip of friendship,
Christmas had made
the bitterest foes friends.

Private Frederick W. Heath **

Opposite me they had one lamp and
9 candles in a row!

Rifleman Ernest Morley - 1/16th Londons ***

** Marian Robson who found and transcribed this account.
*** Extracts from real letters from the Imperial War Museum.

Also by
Hilary Robinson & Martin Impey

by
Hilary Robinson & Martin Impey

ISBN - 978-0-9571245-8-5

by
Hilary Robinson & Martin Impey

ISBN - 978-0-9571245-6-1

For more information about Strauss House Productions
www.strausshouseproductions.com

'Like us' on Facebook - Where The Poppies Now Grow